Hello, Pointy! Are you OK?

No, today I feel sad. I do not want to play.

TINY T. REX

chronicle books · san francisco

AND THE IMPOSSIBLE HUG

by Jonathan Stutzman   illustrated by Jay Fleck

HOW TO MAKE
A FRIEND
FEEL BETTER

•CAKE
•SMILES
HUGS
•TACOS
•JOKES

I have tiny arms.

It is very difficult to hug with tiny arms.

Each day I am growing taller,
but my arms are still tiny.

Hugging almost seems impossible
for a Rex as tiny as me,
but I will try anyway.
Pointy needs me.

Where is my father?

I will ask him for advice.

$3 + 2 = ?$

$7 + 3 = ?$

$5 + 3 = ?$

Rexes are thinkers, not huggers.
Perhaps instead of hugs, mathematics
might be the answer to your problem?

$$x + y$$

$$x + y + z$$

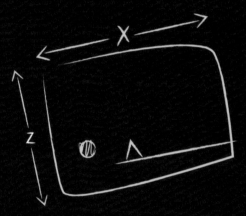

$$\text{happiness} = 8x + 3y + 2z$$

Pointy does not like math.

Math will only make Pointy feel worse.

HELLO,
AUNTIE JUNIP!

I have a problem.
I must learn how to hug, but my arms
are too tiny.

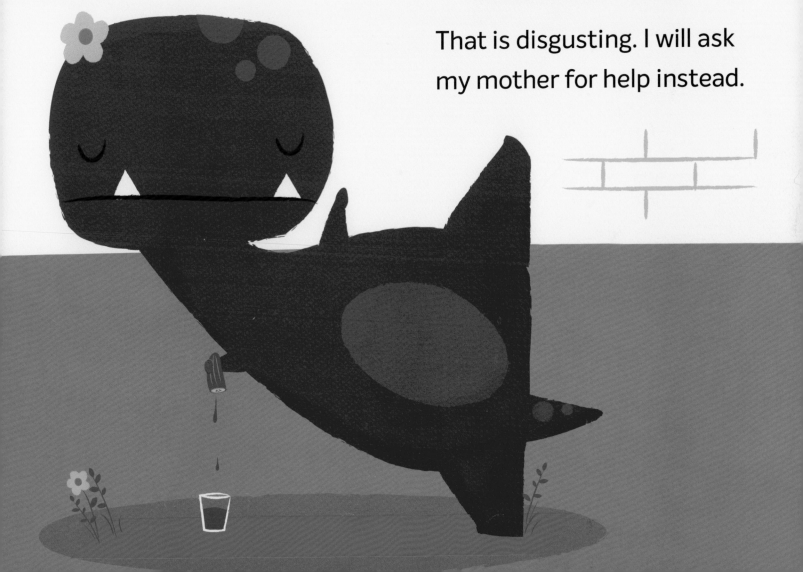

I have found that balance is the key to every problem. Balance and freshly squeezed cucumber juice.

That is disgusting. I will ask my mother for help instead.

I have fallen and now I am lost.

I do not think I will find my
mother in here.

It's okay if you can't hug, Tiny. You are good at many other things. You are kind and creative and braver than most. You are tiny, but your heart is big!

I cannot hug with my heart, Mother.
I must learn to hug with my arms.

HELLO, SISTER!
HELLO, BROTHER!

Please help me.

Hugging is very difficult.

We'd love to help, Tiny!

To do the impossible you must plan and practice.

Practice,

practice,

practice.

Thank you, Trixie and Rawrie. That is good advice.

I will get stronger.

I will practice very hard.
I will practice my hugs on everything!

I will not practice on that anymore.

I am almost ready. I will practice
one more time. When I am done,
I will find my friend.

This tree is very big, like Pointy.
I will hug it.

This is not a tree.
I have made a mistake.
Please help.

From up here, everything looks tiny, like me.
I could hug anything I wanted.

never find

Pointy.

I am here to make you feel better!
I have practiced very hard and hugged
many things.

My arms are still tiny and my hugs are still tiny, but I will do my very best because you are my very best friend.

Thank you, Tiny.

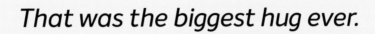

That was the biggest hug ever.

For Fox, my favorite one to hug – J. S.
To anyone that needs a hug – J. F.

Text copyright © 2019 by Jonathan Stutzman.
Illustrations copyright © 2019 by Jay Fleck.
All rights reserved. No part of this book may be reproduced in
any form without written permission from the publisher.

Library of Congress Cataloging-in-Publication Data available.

ISBN 978-1-4521-7033-6

Manufactured in Canada.

FSC
www.fsc.org

MIX
Paper from
responsible sources
FSC® C016245

Design by Jennifer Tolo Pierce.
Typeset in Intelo and Brandon Printed.
The illustrations in this book were rendered in pencil and colored digitally.

10 9 8 7

Chronicle books and gifts are available at special quantity
discounts to corporations, professional associations, literacy
programs, and other organizations. For details and discount
information, please contact our premiums department at
corporatesales@chroniclebooks.com or at 1-800-759-0190.

Chronicle Books LLC
680 Second Street
San Francisco, California 94107

Chronicle Books—we see things differently. Become part
of our community at www.chroniclekids.com.